T0199174

Jean M. Cooper
Illustrated by Pamela Stanley

SOPHIA
the
Piranda

WestBow Press books may be ordered through booksellers or by contacting:

WestBow Press
A Division of Thomas Nelson & Zondervan
1663 Liberty Drive
Bloomington, IN 47403
www.westbowpress.com
844-714-3454

Illustrated by Pamela Stanley

ISBN: 978-1-6642-2521-3 (sc)
ISBN: 978-1-6642-2520-6 (e)

Library of Congress Control Number: 2021903943

Print information available on the last page.

WestBow Press rev. date: 04/07/2021

WestBow
PRESS®
A DIVISION OF THOMAS NELSON
& ZONDERVAN

This book is dedicated to support the education program for the Roma Gypsy children in Romania. It is my hope that it will bring awareness and help combat the social injustice and prejudices that have plagued these people for centuries. All of the proceeds from this book will support the education of Roma and Romanian children. That they may learn to love one another despite their differences under the Cross of Christ. To in turn become all God has called them to be. For more info contact www.beliefinmotion.org

Sophia was a sweet and kind Gypsy girl.

She was a *piranda* (You say it like this: pee-don-da), which means "beautiful Gypsy girl" in Romanian.

Sophia was in the third grade. She lived just outside the big city in a small Gypsy village in Romania.

Sophia walked about a mile to and from school each day.

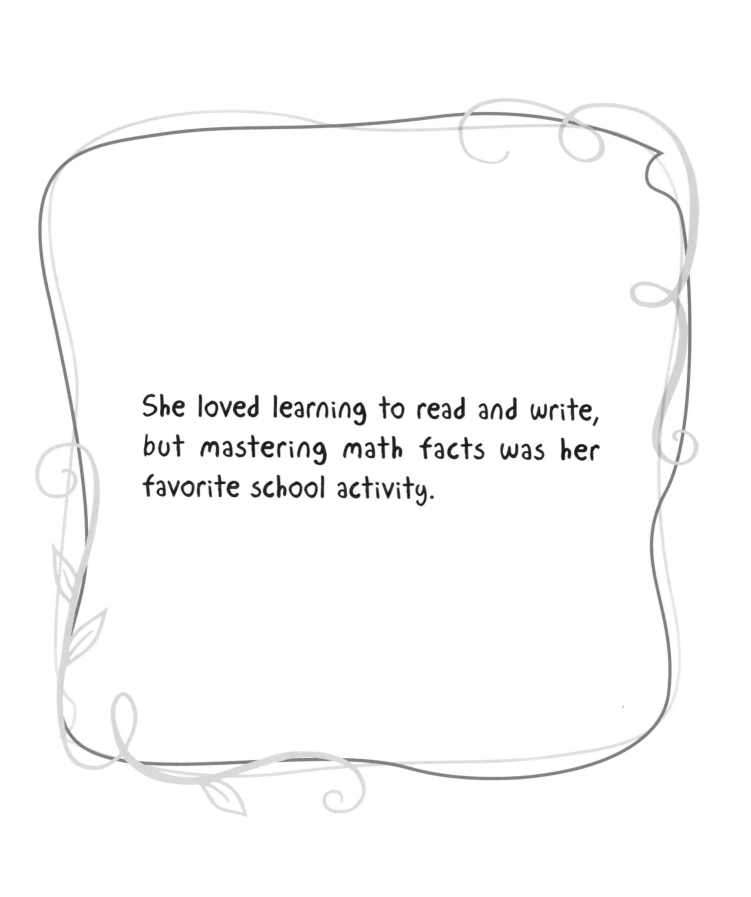

She loved learning to read and write, but mastering math facts was her favorite school activity.

Sophia didn't have any friends because she was a Gypsy and many people did not like Gypsies.

Her classmates weren't very kind. Sophia was often made fun of because she was dirty and sometimes even a little smelly.

Most days, Sophia was sad as she walked home alone.

Her grandmother noticed her sad face as she sat in their yard one day after school. Grandma asked her, "Why are you so sad, my piranda?"

Sophia told her, "I love school, Grandma, and I love to learn, but I have no friends. The other children make fun of me because of where I live. My clothes are old, with holes, and my only shoes are flip-flops. They laugh at me, saying I smell and I'm dirty, but they don't understand, Grandma. We have no water in our homes, and we have no money for new clothes and shoes."

Sophia's grandmother hugged her. With tears in her eyes, she said, "People often say these things because they don't understand. But Jesus teaches us to forgive those who say things against us."

"My piranda, you must trust in Jesus. Continue learning, and master reading, writing, and your math skills. These are the tools that will break the cycle of prejudice. I wish I had done that so you would have a different life."

"I hope you have learned from this. We should never treat others differently. God loves everyone equally, regardless of their skin color and the amount of money they have or don't have. We should always treat people as we would like to be treated. That is what Jesus teaches us."

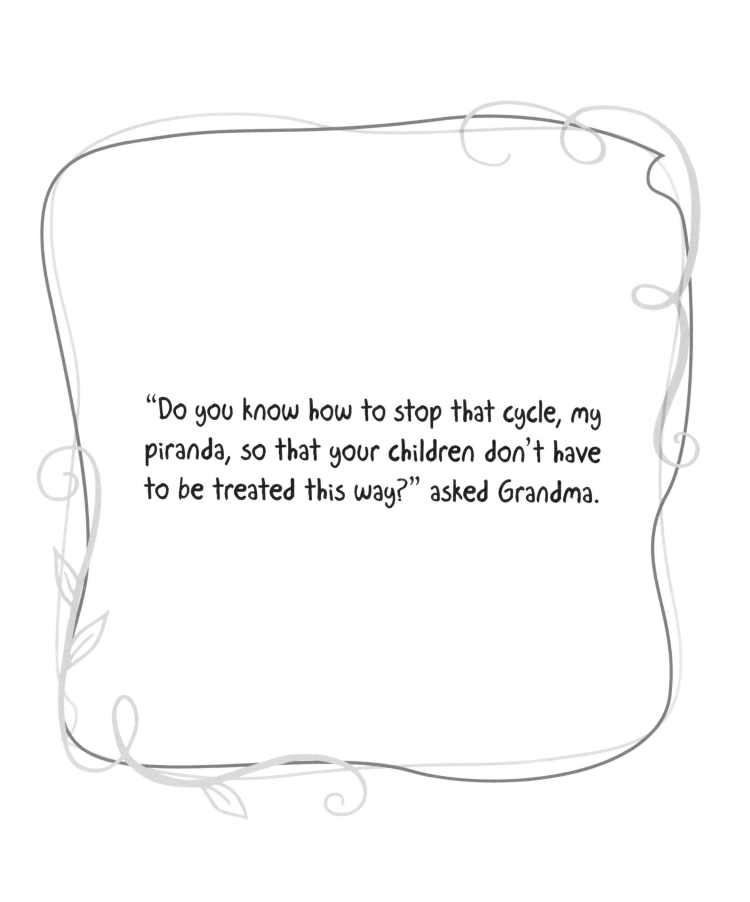

"Do you know how to stop that cycle, my piranda, so that your children don't have to be treated this way?" asked Grandma.

Sophia looked intently and shook her head no.

Grandma said with great love, "Let it start with you. Then you, Granddaughter, can teach others the importance of education. You can be a beautiful example of kindness, a true gift to the world and our God. Jesus has many treasures stored up inside you, so many things He has called you to do. But for today, start here. Despite all the unkindness of others, be kind and diligent in all your work. Then, Sophia, you will be the piranda God has called you to be."

Printed in the United States
by Baker & Taylor Publisher Services